MY
BLEEDING
PARADISE

BUSHRA MAJID

AURAQ

Printed in the Islamic Republic of Pakistan.
Printed: December, 2020
Edition: 1st
ISBN: 978-969-7868-91-9
Price: Rs 800 PKR, $08 US
Illustrations: Ismail Haq

AURAQ
PUBLICATIONS
ISLAMABAD, PAKISTAN

raabta@auraqpublications.com | +92-300-0571-530
www.auraqpublications.com | @AuraqPublications
ISBN : 978-969-7868-91-9

Nourishing tiny buds with blood and sweat,

Watching them grow up, among endless threats.

Then witnessing in front of your eyes,

Them bathing in a barbarous, brutal tint of red.

Yes,

A flower that's taken care of, blooms the best.

Yet it withers before blooming,

And is made a prey of illicit behest.

For years this bloodshed has been going on,

Yet no one pays heed.

Whether it be Syria, Palestine,

Or Kashmir.

(Tehzeeb Sialvi-published in Us magazine-The News)

DEDICATION

A short story with breath taking illustrations to raise voice for our Kashmiri brothers and sisters that will force you to ponder not once but many times and question yourself if any of what has happened and is happening was and is humane in any way?

We share pictures and stories of people afflicted with earthquakes or forest fires. We see help being sent in enormous numbers not just to save humans but animals. Donations worth Millions get collected globally. Why then we fail to publicize the state of desolation that has gripped the inhabitants of the Paradise, we call Kashmir. Nothing can be worse than depriving people from human interaction and cutting them from the rest of the world. Have we failed to understand that this is nothing but severe violation of human rights?

To all the Kashmiris, we stand with you and this is a small effort to prove that!

AUTHOR'S NOTE

I remember asking my Dada what to do about the chaos that keeps flaring up in Kashmir. I had grown up watching all the violence and protests on the tele and so felt desperate for a solution. The wise man told me that we as Pakistanis and Muslims have a huge responsibility towards the Kashmir dispute. As citizens he told me we should contribute not just to the funds but the most important thing was to raise our voices. Being a writer, he knew the impact of words and made me realize my responsibility of doing something about it. Young or adult, it does not matter. Understanding one's obligation and striving towards it is the most realistic approach. The idea for this book was borne right after I had this conversation with him.

Thank you Dada! Always and forever!

I hope Ismail and I have made you proud.

ILLUSTRATOR'S NOTE

When I was a kid, I used to draw a lot and my Nana always encouraged me. He used to send my drawings to children's magazine to get them published and I remember every Saturday going to visit him and finding the latest edition of Young's World, skipping to the drawings' section and finding my piece of art there. It made me happy and he was always very proud. When I got the chance to work on something that could impact and make a difference or at least bring the sufferings of others to light in this cold dark world, I did nothing but to leap on the opportunity. I hope I did justice in telling Bushra's story to the best of my ability and I wish that our Grand Father was here to see this all by himself. He would've been very proud.

Dedicated to the worthiest man of my life, my Nana, Engr. Wajid Naeemuddin.

Darkness behind…………………I'll break free

"Beta! Don't stand near the window! Come on now! Come here!"

But Khansa wouldn't let go! Holding on to the bars so tight, as if trying to break free. There was no view outside to make her long to stand there, glaring into the abyss. There was absolutely nothing to look at…………… Yet everything!

The grip on the window was so firm, it was as if she would break through and emerge out from the suffocating behind!

Hopeful and Hopeless……………………Ironies of life

Khansa was waiting. The big expectant eyes were moving in a saccadic manner, promising to be at peace only when they had found the one they had been looking for.

Baba tum hamesha meray sath ho! -Baba, you are always with me!

She is naïve, her Amma was thinking. Her own throat, dry as a bone, she had no intention to further move her tongue, as even this had become such a big effort, so she kept quiet, having called her once before. She knew Khansa was stubborn but gone were the days when she could play along with the obstinacy of her daughter. She looked at her once more and then lay herself down on the floor, wishing it would all be over soon! Sooner than she had ever wanted!

Oh life! Be hard, but why on a child?

Khansa turned around and saw a blurred shadow of her Amma, cuddled around the far end of the room and probably napping. So, she allowed herself without any hesitation to slightly open the window and look outside. No sound! Even the leaves had frozen in their places. No breeze of wind but the utter flow of dirt and sound as if something had been wrecked and deserted and left abandoned. The world outside looked barren to her and nothing made sense. How could it? She was just six years old and had been part of this life wrecking, jaw dropping and mind- blowing journey since forever! There was no way she could know the normal as there was no normal around. Everything that surrounded her was extreme at all levels. But it was never explained to her why it was the way it was.

It had been 7 days and she missed her friend, best friend. She had not gone to school for almost a week now and for her, it was like in forever! She wondered whether her friend missed her too and the very thought of her was enough to put her into a miserable state.

Just then she felt a strong jerk and sensed a frustrated looking mother pulling her away from the window and shutting it close violently as if telling her *Haven't I forbidden you to do so! Why wouldn't you listen!*

But this has been life here in Kashmir, being pushed and pulled far off the edge of the cliff till life was sucked out of you! She felt miserable! Utter misery!

The sensitive heart deprived her from the carefree childhood!

Seven days before, Khansa was at school in her class, a small yet beautifully decorated grade I room, where she had met some of the greatest people ever. She was hard at work, drawing on the theme "What I want to be when I grow up!"

The teacher was stalking the class room, stopping here and there, every now and then to help anyone who asked for it. But Khansa was too busy to ask for any help. She had a burst of thoughts and ideas circulating in her mind and for her little self, it was too much to put it on a single piece of paper. While the others coloured with markers and colour pencils and crayons, she just had a lead pencil in her tiny hand which she stroked on the paper, sometimes gently, other times a bit aggressively. Finally, the bell rung, and the teacher started to collect the assignment from everyone.

As she went through the art works, she came across many princesses, doctors, engineers, supermen and all sorts of super heroes that one could imagine but none was like Khansa who had wished to become someone who could spread smile and peace across her people. The teacher could sense the sensitive nature of the child and knew that she felt her circumstances and adversity stronger than anyone else in the classroom at such a young age. Only a heart that had been gripped dauntlessly could draw such a concept and she was proud of her little student.

Uncertainty of meeting you again keeps me up at night!

Lunch break had started, and children were running around, chasing each other, and racing towards the canteen. Many could be found in the shades, enjoying their meals and sharing with each other. Khansa and Khizra were also running towards the canteen holding hands tightly. They had barely managed to get into the line when a siren so terrifying started to blow up. It was so loud that if you had not covered up your ears, it would have deafened you in a moment. The shrieking voice coming out of it was terrible and a wave of insecurity and danger had swiped within seconds across the school, the roads and all over the valley.

The crowd broke into a stampede as they all knew what the meaning of that uninvited noise was. Khansa was scared too like everyone else but neither she nor Khizra let go of each other. Instead, they started running in the direction opposite to that of the others, as they feared of getting crushed in the fear-stricken sea of absolutely scared people. Khansa and

Khizra were brave beyond their age. There was no option other than that. It was either bravery or death. Nothing else. The siren meant to clear public places and restrict them to their residences and there was usually no relaxation or tolerance with such things as was evident by the reaction of the innocent people all around.

Some were shouting, others screaming for help, each one trying to reach safety. The girls' decision to go in the other direction proved helpful but only for a short time as they too got lost in the crowd advancing from the opposite side and clinging on to each other now felt the most difficult thing to achieve.

Putting up a fight with a child is no manliness!

The voice of her mother came like a ray of hope amidst the wild chaos all around her and so she tried to lure herself into the direction of the familiar sound. Tearing and making her way through the crowd had drained all her energy but never her spirits. Suddenly, very strong and firmed hands grabbed her by the shoulder and she was terrified to look at her captive. He was the same army man that often so proudly and fearlessly gushed about their valley and killed innocent people. She had heard a lot about these men but never encountered one before. This was her first time. He stared at her and she stared back. She thought she heard her mother's voice calling to her but then a loud "thug" and she felt something rather a million sharp objects piercing her tiny beautiful face, tearing away the soft flesh of her skin and introducing a gush of searing pain right down her spine. The strong grip had loosened now as she shrieked in terror and pain, drawing every eye towards her, who looked at her in equal bewilderment and shock. Just then she felt being lifted by soft gentle hands, caressing her shivering body and soothing her calls of agony with a soft kind tone. Khansa knew that this time it was none other than her own mother.

Bigger the responsibility, Greater the sacrifice!

Earlier that day, when the school had not started yet, Khansa's baba had already left. When she could not find him anywhere around the house, she asked her mother with a look of great concern:

"Amma?"

"Yes!"

"Baba is sleeping?"

"No beta! He has gone out for the march!"

"March? What March Amma?"

"The one we all had been talking about last night! Your baba is going to take part in a proceeding that will raise our voices for our freedom. To uplift the unnecessary curfews, we have been having for so long now!"

"Can I go too?"

"Absolutely not!"

"But why?"

"Because…. It is dangerous! There will be men out there in their uniforms loaded with guns and weapons of who knows what sort. And any wrong move can have dire consequences!"

"But wouldn't it be dangerous for Baba! Shouldn't he not go too?"

"Someone has to go beta! Someone must step up and be the voice of thousands of others. If we don't do this, we may be perished! Come on now, let's get ready for school. You are getting late!"

"Amma you should have woken me up! I wanted to say good bye to him!"

"He already knows, sweet heart! He said his farewell to you when you were fast asleep and left as he was in a hurry!"

"Oh Baba!" Khansa cried and picked up her bag with a heavy heart.

We'll stand... We'll fight... Unsure of the outcomes... But never of the cause!

The big procession was against the unjust captivity of a young lad who had been captured and kept under custody for ten days now. The mob was angry and chanted slogans to release the innocent young man and to stop the torcher immediately. Many of them, including Khansa's father however were not sure if he was even alive. Nonetheless, they stood for each other no matter what.

Soldiers kept throwing tear bombs on them, but their passion was far beyond this to subside. They all wanted to declare to the unjust rule that they cannot do as they please. That they cannot take away whatever they wanted. That human life was sacred and valuable above all. That freedom and liberty were their utmost rights. The people fear nothing as they had been through the most difficult times of their lives.

Suddenly, a wave of commotion spread across the crowd when a man was gunned down and several flairs of blood oozing out of his face and chest could be witnessed. He had been struck by the pellet gun and was badly injured. The anger raised manifold and people could be seen advancing beyond the restricted area. Siren had started to blow out and a situation of emergency was declared across the valley.

The noise was loud and clear. Khansa heard it in her playground. Her mother at home heard it too and made a silent prayer that her husband and daughter return safely. All she could do at that anxious moment was to pray and hope.

The wound gave more pain to the observer than the victim!

Pain! Oh my!

The pain was unbearable. She wanted to rip of her face which had become the source of her pain and a state of indescribable agony. Even the caressing lap of her mother and her sweet "hushes" could not keep her from lying still on the bed. She was at a hospital where her mother had taken her after pulling her from the crowd and had shouted frantically for help. Her wounds had been washed and cleaned but they could not be covered as there was a great chance of them getting infected and so were left open to heal on their own. Her eyes, both, on the other hand, had been covered with a white cloth. During the washing, Khansa had passed out as she felt someone was sprinkling salt on her raw wounds. When she opened her eyes, the sounds of cries and screams welcomed her. She could not hear her mother. There was chaos everywhere. People running. The air held a stench of blood that almost made her nauseated. She could sense everything but was confused.

"Why can't I see?

She asked herself and just as her tiny hands reached to touch the eyes, someone softly took them back and forbade her to do so.

"Amma I can't see!"

"I know beta, I know!"

"Your eyes have been shut! They need time to heal!", her mother sobbed.

Khansa knew something beyond repair had taken place. That it would not be possible to heal from this tragedy after all. Her mother was a strong-willed lady and Khansa had never seen her give up like this. Only a loss so great could shake her core. And just as this thought occurred to her, a wave of horror and terror went chilling down her spine, paralyzing her frail body momentarily, but deeply!

My Blood.... Invaluable.... Any doubt?

Not very far away yet not so near, the procession and the ground had turned into a battle field. People had stones in their hands, some carried sticks but that was about it. Many had been wounded and the crowd was busy to take them for first aid at one hand while keeping the march alive simultaneously. Defeat was a word unknown to them. The army men were under no circumstances willing to release the lad or tell anything about his whereabouts. The father of the boy was the loudest in his chants, demanding the urgent release of his son. Khansa's father repeated his words loud and clear so that the crowd could follow but each passing moment gave the uniformed men more and more anxiety and they all wanted to end this, even if it meant killing anyone. They had orders not to hesitate to push away those who came in their way.

As more and more people got injured, the boy's father grew worried. Finding a chance to grab one of the soldiers, he held him by his collar and shouted for the life of his only son.

Khansa's father was so taken back by this spontaneous action that he ran after him and was just about to reach to his friend when a very sharp thing pierced right through his heart with a very loud bang and he was gone, just like that!

His blood was splattered everywhere and seeing the fate of his beloved friend, the lad's father let go of the soldier's collar and was instantaneously taken into custody.

The crowd hurled stones at the soldiers for they were wounded and angry and grieved by the loss of their people.

Curfew was soon implied across the valley and strict and totally absurd orders had been given out to "kill on spot" if sighted.

The Kashmiris were suffering. The world was watching it on their screens and reading headlines in the newspapers. Talk shows were broadcasted and speeches given in United Nations, yet everything failed to resolve the issue. What the agenda was behind this lack of any purposeful and significant action by the world seemed to have its own motive behind it.

11

His eyes were narrating what and how it had happened!

The hospital had become a refugee camp. Wounded or not, people were pouring in from left and right either to seek help or in hope of finding their loved ones. Khansa wanted to go home. She had been asking her mother for quite some time now, but each time the reply was "no" and she grew more and more disappointed.

Her mother now having listened to the real situation of outside from the people that kept pouring in, was afraid she might not find her husband if they left for home and was hoping he might find his way here in the hospital, so they could be reunited.

Though the curfew had been enforced, people could go from hospital to their houses.

At one side, she was grieve stricken by the loss her daughter had suffered and on the other hand she desperately desired to find her husband.

When several moments had passed and she had no luck finding him, a fearful thought, of him getting lost or captured came over to her and she shivered in utter agony. Just then the sirens could be heard approaching the hospital. They were from the ambulance calling to make way and alert the hospital staff.

A little bit of peace that had started to come back now quickly vanished with the continuous noise of the vehicle and people who could walk went out to look for the source of the commotion.

 Khansa's mother pushed herself through the people to have a peak at the new comers.

The staff was on high alert, making way for the stretcher and pushing people aside. Khansa's mother was so anxious by now that she could not keep herself together and ran towards the men, carrying the stretcher.

"Who is it? Let me see!"

"Madam, please move back! You cannot see him!"

"Please! I beg you! I want to know if it's my husband! He has not come yet!"

"Madam! I am sorry, but you cannot! It's a dead body!"

The words stabbed her tender heart into a million pieces but adamant to make sure it was someone else, she pushed them around and grabbed the cloth to reveal the face and just as she did that, all her fears started coming alive.

She felt nauseated and weak. Her head was spinning, and she felt everything around her turning dark and she wished immensely to perish into the ground, deep within and to never wake up again from this horrifying realization. Realization of the fact that her man had been brutally snatched from her and from her daughter's life forever. She could see it all in his ajar eyes.

Take me with you! Oh Beloved! For if you leave, why should I stay?

Several moments later, time saw them jolting down the uneven road on the back of a cart, pulled by a donkey. There were women and children, all loaded on it, beyond the capacity it could hold. Each one was being carried away from the hospital and towards their homes. Khansa's head was rested upon her mother's lap, who sat motionless, unaffected by the rather harsh journey of the donkey cart. Her eyes were wide open with a fixed gaze, but she was not there mentally. She felt a part of her had died seeing the lifeless body of her husband and was struggling to come to terms with the reality of the situation. How could she? It was not easy. Khansa, due to her bandage could no way comprehend the situation. She was kept unaware of the merciless killing of her father, but she could sense everything. She felt restless in her mother's lap. A lap that had been her safe haven was now not offering the same kind of warmth and comfort. She felt uneasy laying down there and sat down to shake off the feeling of terror that was growing within her with each passing moment.

"Mama!" she shook her lap, but her mother did not answer.

The other women tried to calm her down, but she wouldn't give up until she heard her mother's voice. Little did she know that her mother was not in her senses. That the shock had paralysed her mind and soul and she had forgotten that her daughter lay near her, helpless and wounded!

Terror has turned my smile upside down!

Ten years before, Khansa's parents had gotten married. Khansa would not arrive until after three years. She was there only child, their love, their life! They cherished her birth and very truly grateful of Allah for Blessing them with such a beautiful gift. They protected her as much as possible. With the ongoing terror and a state of uncertainty in the valley, they were sure to be cautious and wary of their surroundings. They, like other people had learnt to survive the bitterness of the unjust capture of their beloved home. It was, however natural to be, at times occupied by uncanny thoughts such as being consistently watched over by equipped men or the befall of yet another massacre or the never-ending unjust enforcement of curfews in the region, jeopardizing their lives.

Khansa had always been a wonderer. When she was very little, she would persistently beg her parents to take her to a park or an open area where she could play. Sometimes, it was very difficult to explain her things, for she would become stubborn and would not eat or drink. Once her father had to go out to buy her biscuits as she would not eat until she got those. When he came back home, he was wounded, blood trickling down his head. Khansa remembered her mother screaming at the horrific condition of her father, running into the kitchen to get a towel. The memory had engrained in her mind and she had never forgotten it. A few years later upon asking her mother she learnt that his father on his way saw the army men beating a youngster for hurling stones at them and so when he had tried to save him, he too had gotten hurt. She was then bitterly reminded by her mother how it was because of her stubbornness that he had to go out.

This was just one memory. Many other like these filled the little child's head and there was a state of chaos and unsafety that had grown within her. She did not have a carefree childhood. She never got the opportunity to be a child. She felt she was born an adult and never a kid. Every other day someone was dying but she could not understand why. Sometimes she had silently wished she had never been born in such an unhappy world!

Serving two purposes; Sight and Vision

The most beautiful thing that Khansa possessed were her eyes. Big and wide like an almond and curious like a kitty. The iris was the perfect ocean green that there ever could be. She had an intense gaze that would cause the beholders to think what she was wondering all the time. How much she wanted the world to know her worries, only she could understand. They all adored her eyes, her Amma, Baba, family and friends, and she felt proud. Her eyes were doors for her happiness and held all the sadness and joys that she had ever seen in her small life.

Now, behind the heavy bandage, the tears had been stained by blood and the beautiful ocean green iris had turned red.

Help me! Shake some sense! Cause I'm dead!

"Munni!" "Munni" Khansa's Mamo was waking her Amma. Little Khansa was confused why he was calling her but waking her Amma. Amma was also the baby of her family and they all called her Munni, just the way Khansa was called so.

"Ummmmmm! Go away" moaned Khansa's Amma.

"I wouldn't! You have to get up now! No more Munni!"

"What for! I am dead" cried her mother.

"Don't say that!" snapped Mamo. "Your Munni can hear you!"

"I am dead! Don't you hear me! I died the day they took him from me!"

"What about this poor child! Who's going to look after her!"

"Help me Bhai!" cried her Amma in desperation.

"I am Munni! You have to get up and take Khansa to hospital!"

"Hospital? What for?" and she got up immediately.

"Her bandages are to be removed today! replied Mamo. "Curfew has been uplifted for a few hours, so we need to hurry!"

Khansa was eager to see again and couldn't wait to please her mum with those ocean eyes.

Please stop before it overflows!

Khansa's eyes were magnified manifold, each time her Amma applied kajal to her. She would do so very generously and Khansa loved to look at herself in the mirror afterwards. She would stare and stare until she could do so no more. She was proud and grateful. Amma would take her "balain"-protection from the evil eye, and baba would take her "bosa"-kiss her, and she would feel the happiest person in the world.

"Baba just imagine how big my eyes will get as I will grow", she had giggled once.

"They wouldn't, Munni However, what can become bigger is your vision, something that you should envision with both your eyes and mind!"

Vision - Envision -- Mind --- Eyes ---- big ----- bigger ------ biggest! And just like that, the bubble being filled with too much worries, concerns and finally violence, bursted. Alas! She could do nothing but stare blankly!

How could she now envision when her pride was not with her anymore? She asked the world, but her voice echoed back to her and she remained unheard and subsequently, unanswered!

Hold on to me as I have nothing left!

Amma dragged herself up. Not that she didn't want to take Munni to the doctor, but she had no strength left in her. Time was running and Mamo was anxious. His cart was outside, ready to go. He gently placed Khansa beside her mum who was as anxious as him for the bandages to be unwrapped. After double checking the lock on the door, he mounted his donkey and raced it to the hospital. Amma's heart was racing all the way as she was dreading to go back to the place where she had found her dead husband. Munni had held her hand tightly as she could sense the pounding beat on her head that was resting on Amma's chest. They both were afraid, neither less than the other, and held onto each other as two lost souls, fearful to lose anything else.

You are braver than me...Stronger than me...but you are only a child my dear!

Baba was looking down at Khansa. He smiled at her.

"Khansa?"

Who is Khansa?

What does that even mean?

Who is calling me?

She opened her ocean and looked up. She couldn't believe. There were no bandages on them. She saw him. Baba. He was there.

Baba is that you?

He nodded and gently stroked her curls.

"Baba yay tum nahe ho!"- Baba this is not you!

She reached out to feel him. He motioned before she could get too close and collected her fingers between the spaces of his own where they had always fitted perfectly. He pulled them closer to his eyes. She wriggled her fingers, wanting to break free of her captivity.

Munni don't, please!

Baba's grip tightened.

One, two three and then countless tears. Her hand was flooded with tears. She knew he was apologizing for leaving her so soon. So, she smiled back at him to let him know that he had been with her always and never left. She had never stopped envisioning him.

"Maaf kardo baita!"- Forgive me child!

"Baba tum sath ho meray hamesha!"- Baba you are always with me!

Always!

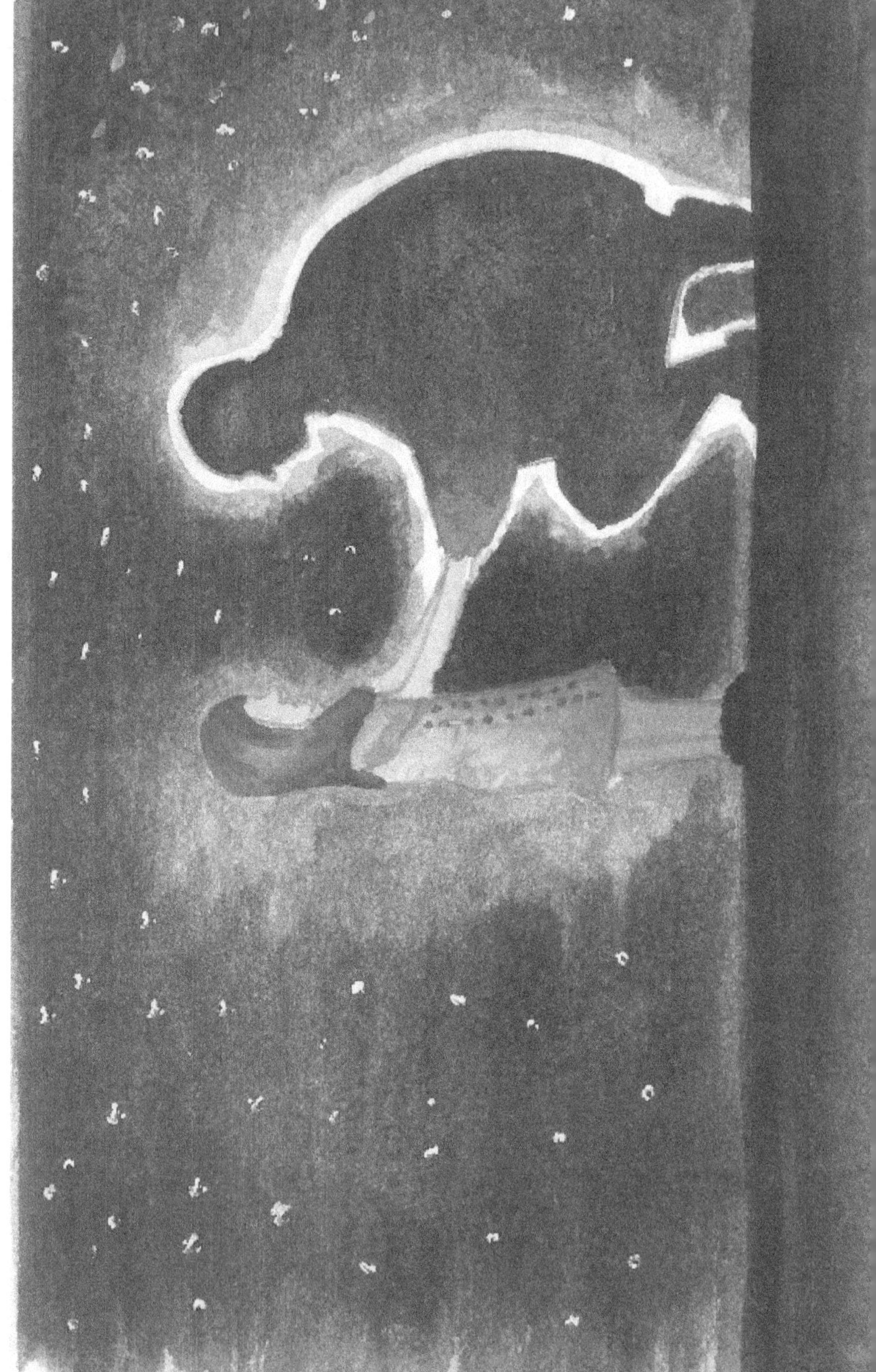

Forgive me my love cause I can't!

Begum Jan! -Dear wife!

UMMMM!

Listen! hushed the voice.

UMMMMM!

Not like this, open your eyes first! Please!

Why?

Why? Because I am requesting you!

But why should I listen to you?

Begum Jan. Maaf kardo! -Forgive me dearest wife!

Nahe! -No!

Allah ka Wasta! -For Allah's sake

Why?

For Munni's sake! Just listen to this once! I will not come back!

Don't you dare say that! And Baba smiled for the first time during their conversation.

Don't you dare leave me like that, cried Amma.

I wouldn't! Take care of yourself. Just look at you! You will not survive one day with what have you done to yourself. My wife was not that weak! For your sake, Munni's and mine.

How are you?

Acha hoon! -I am good! Will be, if you keep praying, forgive me and take care of Munni from both of us!

I will INSHALLAH, hamesha! Allah Willing, Always!

Always!

Your sight is fuel for my love!

The cart had finally halted. Mamo called the Munnis and woke both of them from their sleeps. The valley witnessed them silently smiling!

Connected by heart, blood and soul!

Deja vu!

Swarm of people. War and blood shed never seem to have a break. Hospital was bearing more than it could. Nothing seemed to have changed in the past thirty days that followed the curfew.

They had been waiting a long time for now. But only Mamo looked anxious. The frown on his forehead never seemed to leave. The Munnis on the other hand were deeply absorbed amidst what they had just woken up seeing. It was beautiful, for both of them equally. They all felt connected with the spirit of Khansa's Baba. They were alive on his memories!

Unforgettable!

My vision is bigger than my adversities!

White was approaching. Peace, healing and hope. They had waited for almost 2 hours now, but it was no trouble at all. They were grateful they had a place where they could go with their problems amidst all the clutters and chaos.

Khansa was always confused. She felt it was a waste of time building roads and houses and then bombing them and dumping people to the hospital. At times she wondered why people were even being born when they would be killed mercilessly. How could this place heal anything when all they possessed had been taken away? Was it even possible?

Nothing replaces the loss of a human life!

The doctor smiled as he came towards them.

"Ok then! I will open your bandages now!"

"Yeah!"

"I also have to tell you something, ok?"

"Yeah!" And she felt her each hand taken by Amma and Mamo. They squeezed them hard.

One sticking off. Second and then next and so on. When all was out she felt her head 10 times lighter. Relaxed. She felt she could finally breathe. They seem to have been suffocating her for the past one month.

The voices behind her faded. She knew what the doctor would tell her.

You wouldn't be able to see! -I already know that!

Your face has been scared by the pellets! -I felt the pain and I can still feel them when I run my fingers over my face!

Then, Khansa also wanted to tell the world two things.

Firstly, she sees everything, even now without her eyes.

Secondly, she would live for her Baba, for the people of the Valley. She had already envisioned a beautiful life.

Saw ------ Envisioned ------ Big------ Bigger ------- Biggest!

Always!